STEPHEN HAWKING

MASTERMINDS

IZZI HOWELL

All inquiries should be addressed to:
Peterson's Publishing, LLC
4380 S. Syracuse Street, Suite 200
Denver, CO 80237-2624
www.petersonsbooks.com

All words in **bold** appear in the glossary on page 30.

ISBN: 978-1-4380-8915-7

Printed in China

Picture acknowledgements:
Alamy: Geoffrey Robinson 4, DWD-Media 5, Oxford Picture Library 8, Krzysztof Jakubczyk 10, ©20thCentFox/Courtesy Everett Collection 19, Miguel Sayago 22, Pictorial Press Ltd 24; Getty: Karwai Tang cover, JUSTIN TALLIS/AFP 11, Santi Visalli 15, David L. Ryan/The Boston Globe 16, JIM WATSON/ AFP 17, Gilles BASSIGNAC/Gamma-Rapho 18, Max Mumby/Indigo 25, Chip Somodevilla 26; NASA: 23, Paul Alers 21; Shutterstock: Nicola Pulham 6–7b, Shelly Still Photographer 7tl, aniad 7tr, Vadim Sadovski 9, Maxal Tamor 12 and 30, Andrea Danti 13, Marc Ward 14, Gorodenkoff 20, Belish 27t, Photosite 27bl, Kathy Hutchins 27br, lunamarina 28t, Hadrian 28b, Claudio Divizia 29.
All design elements from Shutterstock.

Every effort has been made to clear copyright. Should there be any inadvertent omission, please apply to the publisher for rectification.

CONTENTS

Who was Stephen Hawking? ~~~ 4

Childhood ~~~ 6

College days ~~~ 8

Family ~~~ 10

Space-time study ~~~ 12

Black holes ~~~ 14

A new voice ~~~ 16

Sharing science ~~~ 18

The future ~~~ 20

Adventures ~~~ 22

The Theory of Everything ~~~ 24

Awards ~~~ 26

Remembering Stephen Hawking ~~~ 28

Glossary ~~~ 30

Further Information ~~~ 31

Index ~~~ 32

WHO WAS STEPHEN HAWKING?

Stephen Hawking was a British **physicist**. He had a brilliant mind and made scientific **breakthroughs** that changed our understanding of **black holes** and the **universe**.

Stephen was diagnosed with **motor neurone disease** in his early twenties. He could not walk or talk for much of his adult life, but he overcame these challenges to continue with his **pioneering** work.

Stephen Hawking is also well-known for his books. His first book, *A Brief History of Time*, was published in 1988 and became a bestseller.

A BRIEF HISTORY OF TIME

FROM THE BIG BANG TO BLACK HOLES

STEPHEN W. HAWKING

INTRODUCTION BY CARL SAGAN

After *A Brief History of Time*, Stephen went on to publish more books.

CHILDHOOD

Stephen was born on January 8, 1942 in Oxford, England. His parents were Frank and Isobel Hawking. He had two younger sisters, named Philippa and Mary, and a brother, named Edward.

The Hawkings were an **eccentric** family. They traveled in an old London taxi and often ate meals together in silence, with each family member reading a book.

In 1950, Stephen and his family moved from Oxford to the city of St. Albans.

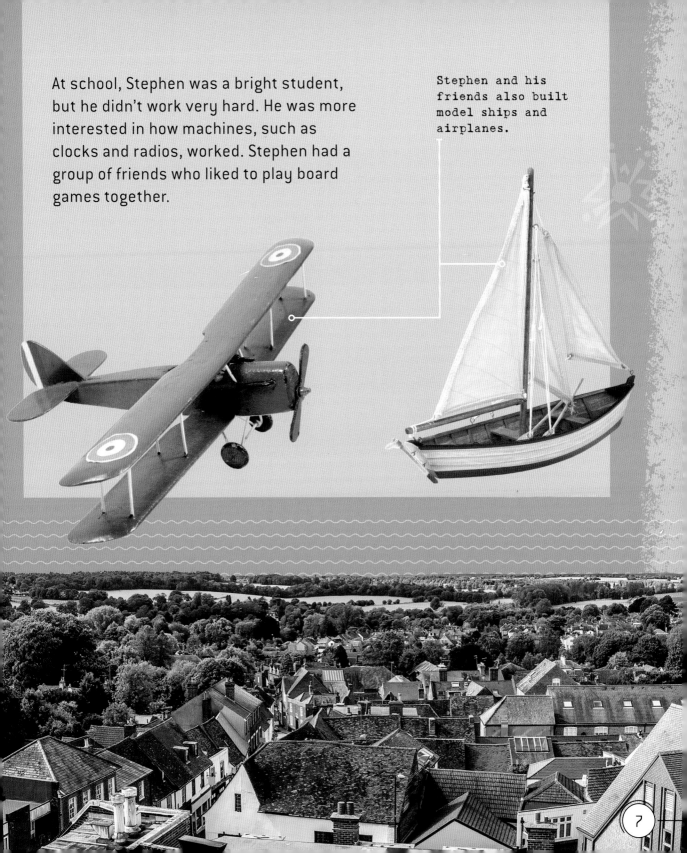

At school, Stephen was a bright student, but he didn't work very hard. He was more interested in how machines, such as clocks and radios, worked. Stephen had a group of friends who liked to play board games together.

Stephen and his friends also built model ships and airplanes.

COLLEGE DAYS

After he finished high school in 1959, Stephen studied physics at the University of Oxford. He had originally wanted to study math, but he wasn't able to because the university didn't offer math as a subject.

Stephen didn't work very hard. However, his intelligence was clear to his teachers, and he **graduated** with a **first class degree**.

Stephen's father, Frank, had also studied at the University of Oxford as a young man. Frank studied medicine.

After his first degree, Stephen did a **PhD** in cosmology (the study of the universe) at the University of Cambridge. While studying there, he was diagnosed with motor neurone disease. This is an **incurable** disease that affects the muscles.

Stephen was told that he only had a few years to live. He focused on his studies, as he wanted to achieve as much as possible in the time he had left. Stephen didn't realize at that time that he would go on to live many years longer than doctors first expected.

Stephen had always been fascinated by the stars as a child. This is one of the reasons why he chose to study cosmology. During his PhD, Stephen studied stars, planets, and galaxies.

galaxy

Stephen met his first wife, Jane Wilde, in 1964. She was a college student who was studying languages. They got married in 1965. They had three children together—Robert, Lucy, and Timothy.

Stephen shows an image of his wedding day at a presentation in 2016.

In 1990, Stephen and Jane got divorced. He later married Elaine Mason, who had been working for him as his nurse. Stephen and Elaine's relationship ended in 2006.

Stephen continued to have a close relationship with Jane, his children, and later, his three grandchildren.

Jane, Stephen, Timothy, and Lucy on the red carpet for an award show for *The Theory of Everything* (see pages 24-25) in 2015.

After Stephen finished his PhD, he started working at Cambridge doing **research**. He was inspired by a mathematician and physicist called Roger Penrose. Roger was researching space-time singularities (places in space where the normal rules of physics do not apply). In the late 1960s, Stephen and Roger started working together and sharing ideas.

The center of a black hole (a **tiny dense** point with huge amounts of **gravity**—see pages 14-15) can be a space-time singularity.

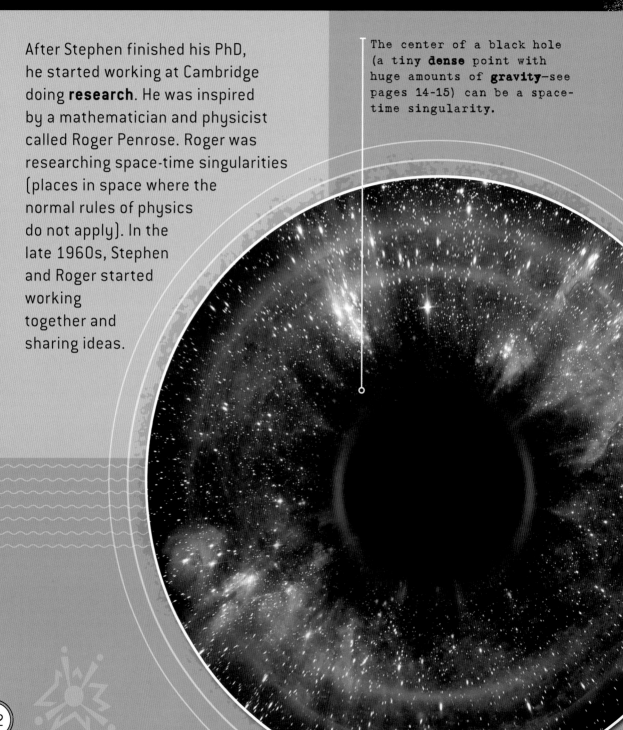

The Big Bang theory (the idea that the universe was created from a single point in a massive explosion) was first suggested in the 1920s and 30s. Roger and Stephen further developed the Big Bang theory using their research about space-time singularities. This helped us to understand more about the beginnings of the universe.

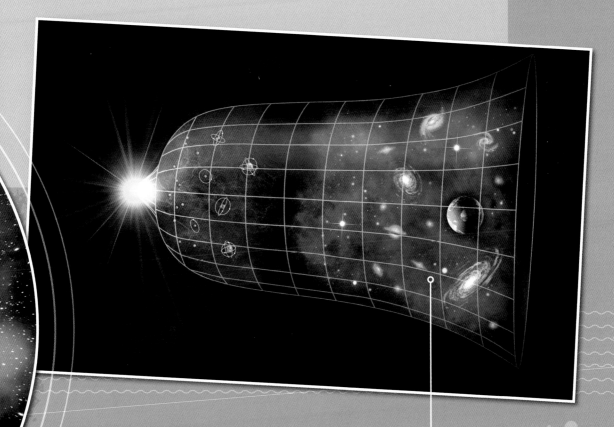

This is a diagram of how the universe formed after the Big Bang. Scientists think that the Big Bang happened about 13.8 billion years ago.

BLACK HOLES

This is an artist's impression of a black hole. It is releasing radiation at the center and pulling in matter from its edges.

After studying space-time singularities, Stephen moved on to studying black holes in more detail. Before this, scientists had thought that nothing could come out of a black hole. However, Stephen's research and calculations suggested that black holes actually release **radiation**.

The radiation released by black holes became known as Hawking radiation, in honor of Stephen. News of Stephen's groundbreaking discovery quickly spread around the world. He was awarded many prizes for his discovery, including the very important role of Lucasian Professor of Mathematics at the University of Cambridge. This is one of the greatest honors for a scientist.

Stephen's newfound fame led to world travel. In this photo, he is visiting Princeton University in New Jersey in 1979.

A NEW VOICE

Stephen wanted to share his scientific ideas and theories with more people by writing a book. However, he had some serious health problems to deal with first. After catching **pneumonia** in 1985, he wasn't able to speak anymore.

In the 1980s, Stephen could still use his hand to control his wheelchair. However, over time, he gradually lost the use of his hands as well.

Stephen found the solution in a computer program that spoke for him. He pressed a switch to choose from a selection of words and phrases. First, he used his hand to select what he wanted to say. Later, he used a muscle in his cheek. Stephen eventually used a word prediction software made especially for him. Stephen used this software to write books and speak to friends and family.

When Stephen gave lectures, his speech would be pre-programmed into his computer.

Thanks to his new computer program, Stephen was ready to start writing his book. *A Brief History of Time* explained complicated science in language that people who aren't scientists could understand. This made his book very popular.

Stephen looks at **translated** French copies of his book. To date, over 10 million copies of *A Brief History of Time* have been sold.

Stephen went on to write many more books about science for the general public. He wrote several books for children with his daughter, Lucy. He also appeared on TV shows, such as *Star Trek*, *The Big Bang Theory,* and *The Simpsons*, as himself. These appearances helped him bring science to more people.

Stephen appeared as an animated character in an episode of the *Futurama* TV show in 2000.

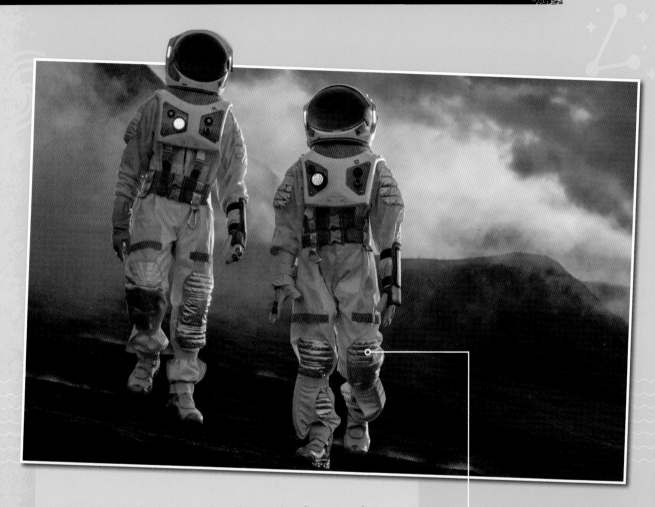

Stephen often thought about the future of space travel. He was very interested in the idea of alien life and supported projects to explore far-off solar systems. However, he was also worried about the risk of meeting aliens that could harm Earth or pass on new diseases.

Stephen hoped that one day, astronauts would explore many different planets.

Stephen was also concerned about the future of life on Earth. He was worried about the risks of **artificial intelligence** and whether, one day, robots could become smarter and more powerful than humans. However, artificial intelligence is not advanced enough for this to happen anytime soon.

Stephen often gave lectures about his theories on the future of space and science. Here, he is giving a speech with his daughter, Lucy.

ADVENTURES

Stephen visited
Antarctica in 1997.

Stephen did not let his disability hold him back. He was very curious about the world around him and traveled to many different places, including South Africa, Chile, and Easter Island. He even went deep underwater in a submarine!

After studying space for so long, it wasn't surprising that Stephen had always dreamed of visiting space. In 2007, he flew in a special aircraft to experience **weightlessness**, as if he were in space. He loved the experience and hoped to travel into space at some point, but sadly he was not able to do so.

The type of airplane that Stephen traveled in to experience weightlessness is nicknamed the "vomit comet," as it usually makes people sick.

THE THEORY OF EVERYTHING

In 2014, a movie called *The Theory of Everything* was released about Stephen's life, his relationship with Jane, and his early work. It was based on a book written by Jane about their relationship.

In *The Theory of Everything*, the actors Eddie Redmayne and Felicity Jones played the roles of Stephen and Jane.

The movie was popular and received lots of awards. Stephen also enjoyed the movie. He allowed the movie makers to use his voice from his computer program to make it more realistic.

Stephen and Jane pose at the movie premiere with Eddie Redmayne and Felicity Jones.

AWARDS

Throughout his life, Stephen Hawking received many awards. He was given thirteen **honorary** degrees from different universities. He was also awarded a **CBE** in 1982 and a Presidential Medal of Freedom in 2009.

President Barack Obama presented Stephen with the Presidential Medal of Freedom.

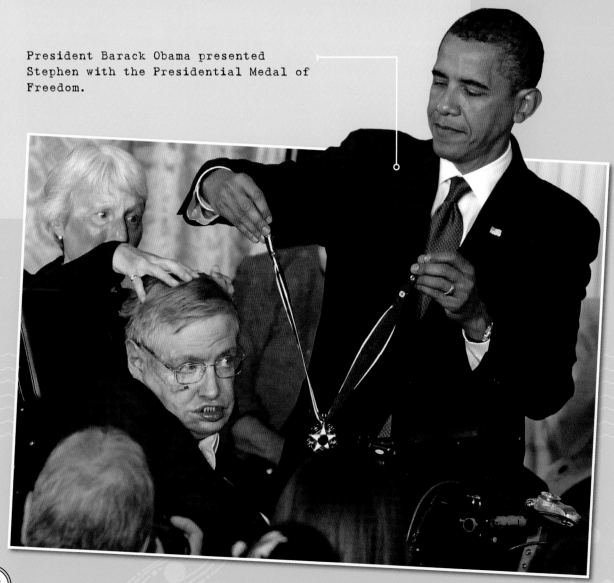

A new award, the Stephen Hawking Medal for Science Communication, was also created in Stephen's honor. This award is for people who help to bring information about science to a wider audience. The first medals were awarded in 2015.

Jim Al-Khalili

Elon Musk

Stephen Hawking Medals for Science Communication have been given to Jim Al-Khalili, a physicist and TV broadcaster who presents TV shows about physics and science, and the technology entrepreneur Elon Musk, the creator of Tesla cars and SpaceX.

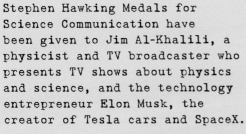

REMEMBERING STEPHEN HAWKING

Stephen Hawking died on March 14, 2018 at the age of 76. People around the world paid their respects and remembered his great achievements.

Stephen's ashes were laid under a stone at Westminster Abbey, London, between the graves of two other pioneering scientists—Isaac Newton (1642-1727) and Charles Darwin (1809-1882).

Newspapers around the world reported Stephen Hawking's death.

Gonville and Caius College
The Stephen Hawking Building
and **Harvey Court**
Visitors must report to Porters' Lodge
CCTV IN OPERATION
IMAGES ARE BEING RECORDED FOR THE DETECTION AND PREVENTION OF CRIME AND PUBLIC
SAFETY BY GONVILLE & CAIUS COLLEGE AND WILL BE SHARED WITH OTHER AGENCIES AS
REQUIRED BY LAW OR TO MAINTAIN PUBLIC SAFETY OR DETECT CRIME
FOR FURTHER INFORMATION, CONTACT 01223 335400

We will always remember Stephen Hawking for his incredible mind, his contribution to science, his dedication to his work, and for overcoming his physical challenges. He helped to bring science to a wider audience and engage people with the wonders of the universe.

He was also a role model for disabled people. He helped to raise awareness of their rights and raised money for charities that support disabled people.

A building at the University of Cambridge was named after Stephen Hawking to honor him.

GLOSSARY

artificial intelligence: The ability of robots or computers to think like humans do

black hole: A region in space with a very strong gravitational pull

breakthrough: An important discovery that provides an answer to a problem

CBE: An important award given in the UK

dense: With parts that are closely packed together

eccentric: Strange and unusual

first class degree: The highest level qualification given after completing a college course

graduate: To complete a college course and receive a degree

gravity: A force that pulls objects together

honorary: Describes a degree given to someone as an honor or reward

incurable: Unable to be cured

motor neurone disease: An incurable disease that affects the muscles

PhD: The most advanced qualification from a college or university

physicist: Someone who studies the way the physical world works

pioneering: Starting the development of something important

pneumonia: A serious disease that affects the lungs

radiation: Energy in the form of waves or particles

research: Studying something in order to gather more information about it

translated: Changed into another language

weightlessness: The feeling of not being affected by gravity, as experienced in space

universe: Everything that exists, including all of the stars and planets in space

TIMELINE

1942
Stephen Hawking is born in Oxford, England.

1959
Stephen begins his first degree in physics at the University of Oxford.

1962
Stephen starts his PhD in cosmology at the University of Cambridge.

1963
Stephen is diagnosed with motor neurone disease.

1964
Stephen marries Jane Wilde.

Late 1960s
Stephen and Roger Penrose research space-time singularities together.

FURTHER INFORMATION

BOOKS

The Big Bang and Beyond (Planet Earth)
by Michael Bright (PowerKids Press, 2017)

Who Was Stephen Hawking?
by Jim Gigliotti (Penguin Workshop, 2019)

The Story of Space
by Catherine Barr and Steve Williams (Frances Lincoln, 2017)

WEBSITES

www.natgeokids.com/uk/discover/science/general-science/stephen-hawking-facts/
Discover ten fun facts about Stephen Hawking.

www.ted.com/talks/stephen_hawking_asks_big_questions_about_the_universe?language=en
Watch a speech made by Stephen Hawking about the universe in 2008.

www.bbc.co.uk/bitesize/topics/zd4dy9q/articles/zjkp8xs
Learn more about the life of Stephen Hawking and test your memory with an activity about his life.

1979
Stephen becomes Lucasian Professor of Mathematics at Cambridge.

1988
A Brief History of Time is published.

1990
Stephen and Jane get divorced.

2009
Stephen is awarded the Presidential Medal of Freedom.

2014
The movie *The Theory of Everything* is released.

2018
Stephen dies at the age of 76.

INDEX

A Brief History of Time, 5, 18

aliens, 20

artificial intelligence, 21

awards, 11, 15, 25–27

Big Bang Theory, 13

black holes, 4, 12, 14–15

books, 5–6, 16–19, 24

childhood, 6–7

death, 28

family, 6, 8, 10–11, 19, 21, 24

Hawking radiation, 15

Hawking, Lucy, 10–11, 19, 21

Hawking, Robert, 10

Hawking, Timothy, 10–11

Mason, Elaine, 11

motor neurone disease, 4, 9

Penrose, Roger, 12–13

PhD, 9, 12

space-time singularities, 12–14

Stephen Hawking Medal for Science Communication, 27

The Theory of Everything, 11, 24–25

travels, 22

TV shows, 19, 27

universe, 4, 9, 13, 29

University of Cambridge, 9

University of Oxford, 8

weightlessness, 23

wheelchair, 16

Wilde, Jane, 10–11, 24–25

word prediction software, 17

More titles in the the **Masterminds** series

- Who was Rachel Carson? • Childhood • University life • Under the sea • Writing and books • Marine research • Pesticides • Silent Spring • Speaking out • Death • The green movement • Remembering Rachel Carson • Our environment today

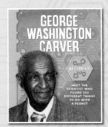

- Who was George Washington Carver? • Childhood • Freedom • Getting an education • Farm studies • New crops • Peanut products • The sweet potato • Making a change • Colourful dyes • Honours • Later life • Remembering Carver

- Who was Marie Curie? • Childhood • Studies in France • Meeting Pierre • Studying rays • New discoveries • Radioactive radium • Working hard • Family • Teaching and learning • The First World War • Later years • Remembering Marie Curie

- Who was Rosalind Franklin? • Childhood • University • The Second World War • Working in France • DNA • A new job • Photographic evidence • Studying viruses • Forgotten work • Illness • Celebrating Rosalind Franklin

- Who is Jane Goodall? • Childhood • Off to Africa • Ancestors and evolution • Living with chimpanzees • New discoveries • Back to school • Family • Inspiring others • Books • The Jane Goodall Institute • Activism • Celebrating Jane Goodall

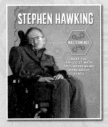

- Who was Stephen Hawking? • Childhood • University days • Family • Space-time study • Black holes • A new voice • Sharing science • The future • Adventures • *The Theory of Everything* • Awards • Remembering Stephen Hawking

- Who is Katherine Johnson? • Bright beginnings • Getting ahead • Teaching and family • A new job • Fighting prejudice • Into space • In orbit • To the Moon • Later life • *Hidden Figures* • Celebrating Katherine Johnson • A new generation

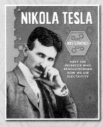

- Who was Nikola Tesla? • Childhood • Growing up • Electricity and Edison • Moving to the USA • Branching out • The war of the currents • New projects • Wireless power • Struggles • Awards • Later life • Remembering Tesla

- Who was Leonardo da Vinci? • Early life • Working in Milan • Famous paintings • Body sketches • Back to Florence • The Mona Lisa • Animal sketches • Flight sketches • Military sketches • Engineering sketches • The later years • Remembering Leonardo

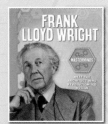

- Who was Frank Lloyd Wright? • Childhood • Education • Off to Chicago • Family • First designs • Prairie houses • Building details • A new home • Teaching • Famous buildings • Later life • Remembering Frank Lloyd Wright